Hairy Maclary's
caterwaul caper

Lynley Dodd

Spindlewood

With a twitch of his tail
and a purposeful paw,
down by the river
crept Scarface Claw.

He woke up a lizard,
he startled a bee,
and he bothered a blackbird
high in a tree.

Higher and higher
he sneakily snuck,
but up in the branches
he suddenly
STUCK.
'WROWWW-W-W-W-W-W-W,'
he yowled.

Hairy Maclary
was eating his meal;
jellymeat,
biscuits,
a snippet of veal.
All of a sudden
he heard a STRANGE sound;
a yowling,
a wailing
that echoed around,
'WROWWW-W-W-W-W-W-W.'
'YAP-YAP-YAP,'
said Hairy Maclary,
and off he went.

Hercules Morse
was asleep in a glade,
with his tail in the sun
and his head in the shade.
THEN came the sound
that echoed around,
'WROWWW-W-W-W-W-W-W.'
'WOOF,'
said Hercules Morse,
and off he went.

Bottomley Potts
was rolling about,
with his feet in the air
and his tongue hanging out.
THEN came the sound
that echoed around,
'WROWWW-W-W-W-W-W-W.'
'RO-RO-RO-RO-RO,'
said Bottomley Potts,
and off he went.

Muffin McLay
was having a bath,
in the old wooden tub
at the side of the path.
THEN came the sound
that echoed around,
'WROWWW-W-W-W-W-W-W.'
'RUFF-RUFF,'
said Muffin McLay,
and off he went.

Bitzer Maloney
was having a scratch,
as he lay in the sun
in the strawberry patch.
THEN came the sound
that echoed around,
'WROWWW-W-W-W-W-W-W.'
'BOW-WOW-WOW-WOW,'
said Bitzer Maloney,
and off he went.

Schnitzel von Krumm
was digging a hole,
in his favourite spot
by the passionfruit pole.
THEN came the sound
that echoed around,
'WROWWW-W-W-W-W-W-W.'
'YIP-YIP,'
said Schnitzel von Krumm,
and off he went.

Puffing and panting
impatient to see,
together they came
to the foot of the tree.
They sniffed and they snuffled,
they bustled around,
and they saw WHAT was making
the terrible sound.

'YIP-YIP,'
said Schnitzel von Krumm.
'BOW-WOW-WOW-WOW,'
said Bitzer Maloney.
'RUFF-RUFF,'
said Muffin McLay.
'RO-RO-RO-RO-RO,'
said Bottomley Potts.
'WOOF,'
said Hercules Morse.
'YAP-YAP-YAP,'
said Hairy Maclary
and...

'*WROWWW-W-W-W-W-W-W,*'
said Scarface Claw.
The din was so awful
that up hill and down,
you could hear the CACOPHONY
all over town.

Miss Plum brought a ladder
and climbed up the tree.
She rescued old Scarface;
at last he was free.

With a flick of his tail
and a shake of each paw,
off at a gallop
went Scarface Claw.

And back to their business
and Donaldson's Dairy,
went all of the others
with Hairy Maclary.

British Library Cataloguing in Publication Data
Dodd, Lynley
  Hairy Maclary's caterwaul caper
  1. Title
  823[J] PZ7.

Other Lynley Dodd books

MY CAT LIKES TO HIDE IN BOXES (with Eve Sutton)
THE NICKLE NACKLE TREE
TITIMUS TRIM
THE APPLE TREE
THE SMALLEST TURTLE
HAIRY MACLARY FROM DONALDSON'S DAIRY
HAIRY MACLARY'S BONE
HAIRY MACLARY SCATTERCAT
WAKE UP, BEAR

Published in 1987 by Spindlewood
70 Lynhurst Avenue, Barnstaple, Devon EX31 2HY.

First published in 1987 by
Mallinson Rendel Publishers Ltd.
Wellington, New Zealand.

Reprinted January 1989

ISBN 0-907349-91-9

Printed and bound by Colorcraft Ltd., Hong Kong.